Larry Gets Lost in Seattle

Illustrated by John Skewes
Written by John Skewes and Eric Ode

little bigfoot
an imprint of sasquatch books
seattle, wa

For Mother and Father

Special thanks to Robert Schwartz, there at the beginning

Manufactured in China by C&C Offset Printing Co. Ltd. Shenzhen, Guangdong Province, in November 2016

Published by Little Bigfoot, an imprint of Sasquatch Books

21 20 19 18 17   9 8 7 6 5 4 3 2 1

Editor: Christy Cox
Production editor: Em Gale
Design: Mint Design

Library of Congress Cataloging-in-Publication Data is available.

ISBN: 978-1-63217-092-7

Sasquatch Books
1904 Third Avenue, Suite 710
Seattle, WA 98101
(206) 467-4300
www.sasquatchbooks.com
custserv@sasquatchbooks.com

This is **Larry.** This is **Pete.**
They ride together in the back seat.

They come to the water,
but cars cannot float.
So Dad drives them onto
a big ferry boat.

The boy and his dog
stand and watch from the rail.
Pete knows where they're going.
Larry's wagging his tail.

WASHINGTON STATE FERRIES
Back and forth, back and forth. Every day, ferry boats carry
people, cars, buses, and bicycles across Puget Sound.

Seattle Great Wheel

The ferry boat docks
with a creak and a rattle.
"Let's go!" hollers Pete.
"We are here in Seattle!"

Seattle

SMITH TOWER
Once upon a time, Smith Tower was the tallest building in Seattle. But look at it now!

Pioneer Square

The first place they visit
has so much to see,
a tower of animals
carved from a tree.

A roof made of steel,
and then, there, all alone,
a wise-looking man
who's been carved out of stone.

Chief Seattle by James Wehn

Now Larry is hungry.
And what has he found?
A yummy surprise
waiting here on the ground.

A gobble. A chomp.
Then a jungle of feet.

When Larry looks up,
there is no sign of Pete!

So Larry finds stairs,
and he follows them down.
But Pete isn't here
in this underground town.

UNDERGROUND TOUR
What's hiding below Pioneer Square?
Old Seattle! You can find signs, storefronts,
and even the city's oldest toilet.

CenturyLink Field

915

12

Above, he hears whistles.
A train is appearing.
And somewhere a large crowd
of people are cheering.

A giant might help him,
he thinks, looking up.
But this one's too busy
to help a lost pup.

SEATTLE • ART • MUSEUM

HAMMERING MAN
What a hard worker! At forty-eight feet tall, the
Hammering Man, created by Jonathan Borofsky,
hammers from 7 a.m. to 10 p.m. every day except
Labor Day.

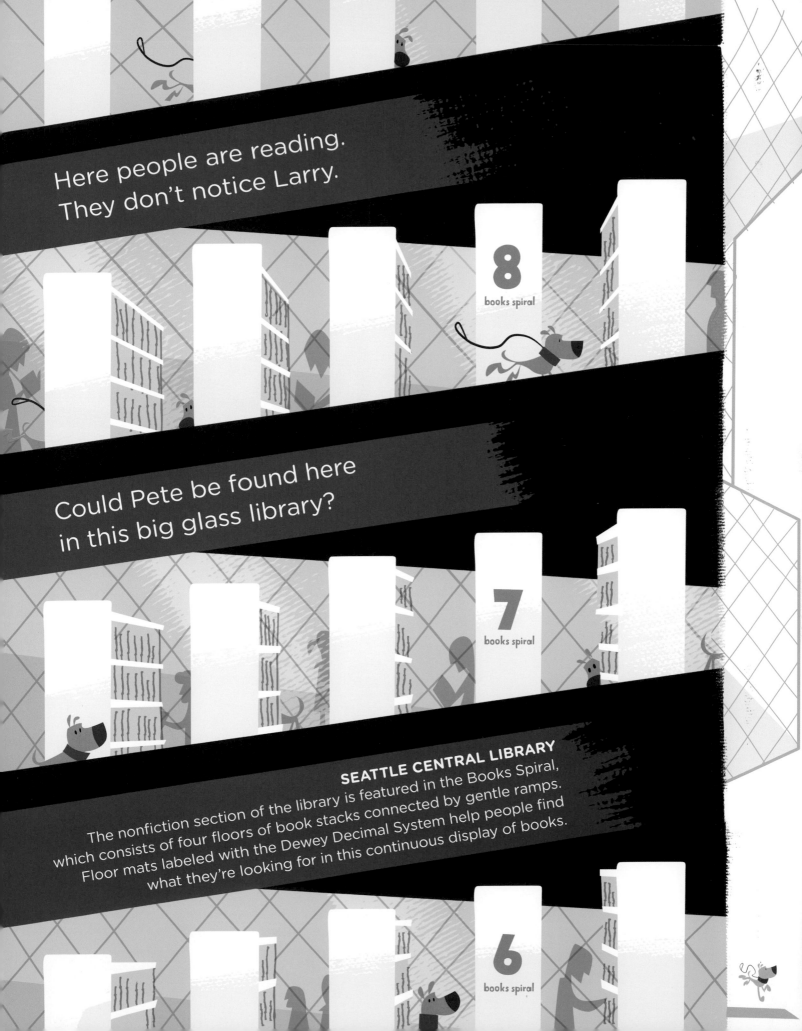

Here people are reading.
They don't notice Larry.

8 books spiral

Could Pete be found here in this big glass library?

7 books spiral

SEATTLE CENTRAL LIBRARY

The nonfiction section of the library is featured in the Books Spiral, which consists of four floors of book stacks connected by gentle ramps. Floor mats labeled with the Dewey Decimal System help people find what they're looking for in this continuous display of books.

6 books spiral

PUBLIC
MARKET
CENTER

FARM

NEWS

报纸

新闻

He comes to a market
with good things to eat,
and flowers and music
and people to meet.

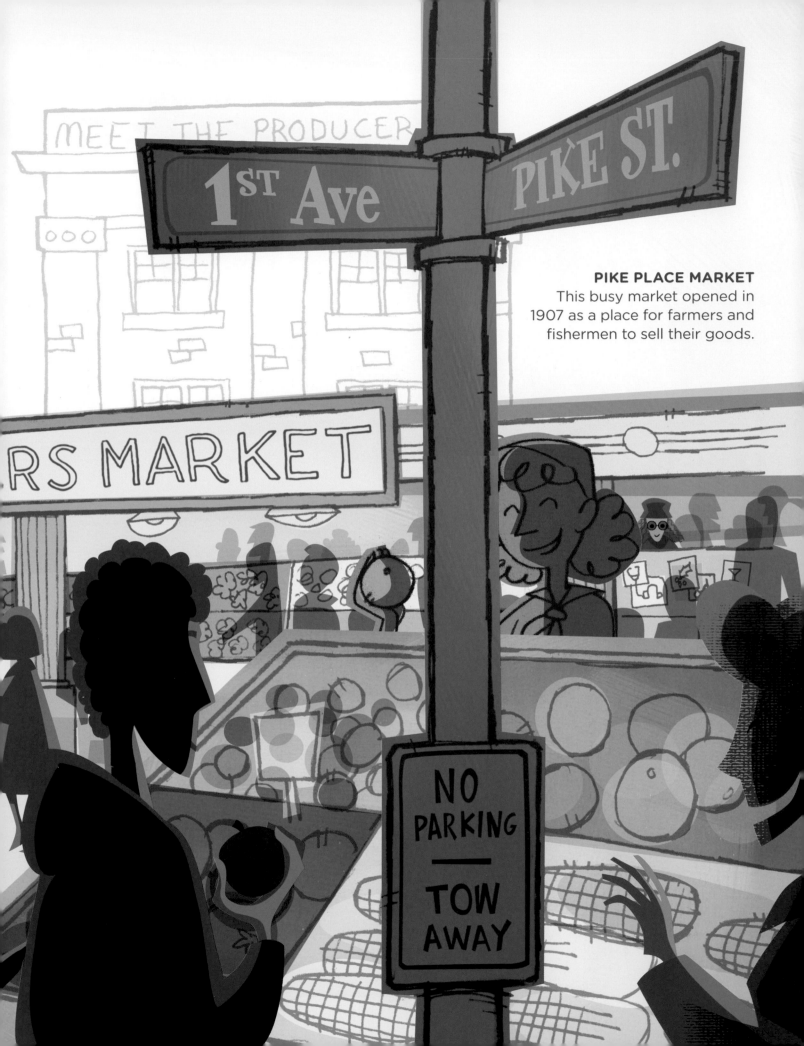

PIKE PLACE MARKET
This busy market opened in 1907 as a place for farmers and fishermen to sell their goods.

He reaches a park
where nothing seems right.

The Eagle by Alexander Calder

A bird, tall and sturdy,
with wings like a kite.

Eye Benches by Louise Bourgeois

A tree like a mirror,
all shiny and bright.

Split by Roxie Paine

Schubert Sonata by Mark di Suvero

Monorail

He finds a tall tower,
like something from space.
A train races by
from some high-above place.
But nowhere does Larry
see Pete's friendly face.

Space Needle

SEATTLE CENTER
The Seattle Center is packed with museums and theaters. The monorail, the International Fountain, and the saucer-shaped Space Needle were all built for the 1962 World's Fair.

EMP Museum

Seaplane

U.S. MAIL M92

N-ABNA

Lincoln's Toe Truck

He hurries past ships
and then in through a door.
This place looks like nowhere
he's been to before.

With airplanes and boats
hanging high in the air,
it's a fun place to visit,
but Pete isn't there.

Gas Works Park

MOHAI

At the Museum of History and Industry, you can see the glue pot that accidentally started Seattle's Great Fire in 1889. When Seattle was rebuilt, it quickly grew from being a small town to a major city.

Hydroplane

U-27 Slo-mo-shun IV

Lumber Truck

And here is a park
with machines on the ground.
But parks aren't much fun
when your friend's not around.

Fremont

Waiting for the Interurban
by Richard Beyer

Late for the Interurban
by Kevin Pettelle

He meets other people,
some funny, some scary.
But no one, it seems,
wants to help little Larry.

Fremont Troll
by the Jersey Devils

N 34th St

◀ Troll Ave N 900

P. Patches Pl

LAKE UNION HOUSEBOATS
If you lived in a floating home on Lake Union, you
could go fishing out your bedroom window!

Then here, where the houses
each float like a duck,
an odd looking creature
has poor Larry stuck.

Larry leaps from the dock,
and he lands in the lap
of a fishing boat captain
who's taking a nap.

He checks Larry's collar,
then places a call.
"Hang on," says the man.
"This won't take long at all."

They sail past a bridge,
and a short moment later,
the boat starts to drop
like a strange elevator.

Aurora Bridge

Fremont Bridge

BALLARD LOCKS
Boats travel from Lake Union to the Puget Sound through these giant locks. Heavy gates keep the salty ocean water from mixing with the fresh lake water.

Poor Larry is worried.
He can't wait much more.
Then who does he see
up ahead on the shore?

ALKI BEACH
Do you remember the statue of Chief Seattle at the beginning of Larry's adventure? When the first settlers landed at Alki Beach in 1851, Chief Seattle and his tribe helped them build a cabin for the winter.

It's Larry's friend Pete!
Larry lets out a bark.
They dance and they hug,
as the evening grows dark.

They climb in the car,
and they buckle up tight.
Then Larry and Pete
wish the city goodnight.

Get More Out of This Book

Meet My Town

Because of its rainy climate and unique location on the water, the city of Seattle has a very distinctive "personality." Ask readers what sort of personality their town has. How is their town different from Seattle? Does it have beaches, ferry boats, or houseboats? How is it similar to Seattle? Does it have a farmers' market or a baseball field?

One or the Other

Have readers write or dictate a short piece comparing the most interesting thing in their town with the most interesting thing in Seattle, based on their reading of the book. Why did they choose the things they did?

Building Blocks

Seattle has some unusual buildings and public structures as portrayed in the book: the Space Needle, the EMP Museum, the Fremont Troll, the Hammering Man. Ask readers to think of any other unusual buildings they've seen or heard about. How would they describe those buildings? Have readers design and draw their own "crazy building," show it to the class, and explain how they came up with the idea.

TEACHER'S GUIDE: The above discussion questions and activities are from our teacher's guide, which is aligned to the Common Core State Standards for English Language Arts for Grades K to 1. For the complete guide and a list of the exact standards it aligns with, visit our website: SasquatchBooks.com